THIS WALKER BOOK
BELONGS TO:

First published in *Fairy Tales* 2000 by Walker Books Ltd
87 Vauxhall Walk, London SE11 5HJ

This edition published 2010

2 4 6 8 10 9 7 5 3 1

Text © 2000 Berlie Doherty
Illustrations © 2000 Jane Ray

The right of Berlie Doherty and Jane Ray to be identified respectively
as the author and illustrator of this work has been asserted by them
in accordance with the Copyright, Designs and Patents Act 1988

This book has been typeset in Palatino

Printed in China

British Library Cataloguing in Publication Data:
a catalogue record for this book is available from the British Library

ISBN 978-1-4063-2976-6

www.walker.co.uk

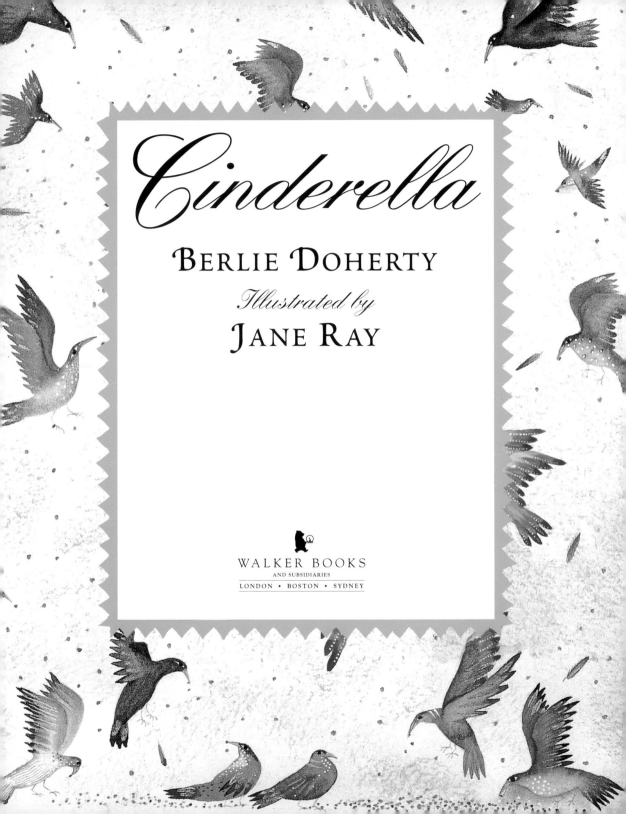

Cinderella

BERLIE DOHERTY

Illustrated by

JANE RAY

WALKER BOOKS
AND SUBSIDIARIES
LONDON • BOSTON • SYDNEY

There was once a girl who lived with her father and his new wife and her two daughters. Her mother had died, and the new wife was jealous because the girl missed her mother so much, and because she was prettier than her own daughters. She tried to hide her away at the bottom of the house. And the sisters had such ugly hearts that they treated the girl as if she was their servant. They came to be known as the ugly sisters.

The girl had to do everything for them, and never got any thanks for it. All she had to wear was a ragged grey dress, and at night when her work was done, she had to sleep on the hearth among the ashes and the cinders. And so she became known as Cinderella.

One day Cinderella's father was going on a journey, and he asked his three daughters what they would like him to bring back for them.

"Oh, some glittery gold to wear round my neck!" said the oldest.

"Oh, some sparkly jewels to match my eyes!" said the second.

The father smiled fondly and said to Cinderella, "And what about you?"

"I would like the first twig that

brushes against your hat as you ride," said Cinderella.

Her sisters laughed in scorn.

"The girl's an idiot!" the stepmother said. "She doesn't even deserve a present!"

So when the father came home again he had gold and jewels and a twig from a hazel tree in his bag, and straight away Cinderella ran outside with her twig and stuck it in the earth on her mother's grave, and wept over it.

Every day, if Cinderella had a little time for herself in between all her chores, she would steal out to the twig and nourish it with her tears, and it wasn't long before something wonderful happened. The hazel twig started to grow. It began to put out spindly little branches, and buds sprouted on the branches, and green leaves unfurled from the buds. It became a tree. Its leaves danced and fluttered in the wind, and wrens and blackbirds and thrushes and turtle-doves all settled in its branches and sang to her.

Soon after this had happened there came an announcement that the Prince of the Realm was to hold a three-day feast, with a magnificent ball on each of the three nights, and that at the end of the three days he was going to choose his bride. Imagine the excitement at Cinderella's house when the invitations arrived!

"At last, at last!" the stepmother said to her husband. "He's bound to choose one of our daughters!"

The two ugly sisters were full of it. It was all they could talk about, and they squabbled all the time over which of them was most likely to be chosen by the prince. They ordered Cinderella to make ball-gowns for them, and they paraded in front of the looking-glass, scowling at what they saw and blaming Cinderella for everything.

"Too long!"

"Too short!"

"Too tight!"

"Too loose!"

"Too plain!"

"Too flouncy!"

"Can't you do anything right!" her stepmother shouted.

When there was no more material to

be used up and the night of the first ball was upon them, they told Cinderella that her efforts would have to do. Not a word of thanks, of course.

"Now you can do our hair," they said. "Make us look beautiful, and be quick

about it!"

They were asking the impossible, of course, but Cinderella did her best, and when all this was done, she said to her stepmother, "What can I wear to the ball?"

Her stepmother was so astonished that she nearly forgot how to speak. "You!" she said. "Who said anything about you going to the ball?"

"But the invitation was for all of us. Please let me go!" Cinderella turned to her father. "Please let me!"

And this is what the stepmother did, to keep her quiet. She picked up a bowl of rice and flung it into the ashes of the fire. "Pick out all those grains of rice," she told her, "and then you may go to the ball."

She went upstairs with her two daughters, and they put on their ball-gowns.

Cinderella ran out of the kitchen to her hazel tree and called up to it,

"Hazel tree, hazel tree,
Will you help me?"

Instantly there was a chirruping and cooing and a fluttering of wings, and her wrens and her thrushes and blackbirds and her turtledoves all flew down to her. They picked and pecked through the ashes and in no time at all there was a bowl of clean rice grains with all the ashes shaken off.

Singing with excitement, Cinderella

ran to show her stepmother. "Now I can go to the ball!" she said.

Her stepmother didn't even look at the bowl of rice in Cinderella's hands. "Don't be ridiculous! In that tatty dress! You can't even dance! It's out of the question."

Cinderella begged and pleaded so much that this is what the stepmother did. She took *two* bowls of lentils and threw them into the ashes. "Pick those out, clean enough to eat, and you can go to the ball," she said, and she and her daughters started putting on their gloves and their dancing slippers.

So once more Cinderella ran out of the kitchen to her hazel tree and called up to its branches,

"Hazel tree, hazel tree,
Will you help me?"

Instantly there was a chirruping and a fluttering of wings and her wrens and her thrushes and blackbirds and her turtledoves picked and pecked through the ashes to find all the lentils, and shook them till they were clean enough to eat.

Full of joy, Cinderella ran out of the kitchen with the bowls. Her stepmother and sisters were just about to step into the carriage. The horse was stamping his hooves, ready to be off. "Wait!" Cinderella called. "I've done it! I can go now!"

But her mother and her sisters laughed, and didn't even look at the bowls of lentils.

"Look at you! You're a bundle of rags! How can you possibly go to the ball?"

Cinderella clung on to her father's hand. "Please let me go!" But her step-mother took up the reins and the carriage swept away.

Cinderella was left alone in the house. Sad and sighing, she went out to her hazel tree and sat underneath it.

"Hazel tree, hazel tree,
Will you help me?"

She heard a fluttering as if all the leaves were unfurling at once, and the birds of the tree flew down carrying a silver dress and slippers that glittered like stars. Cinderella put them on, and ran to the ball.

The palace was glowing with coloured streamers and candlelight. Beautiful ladies swayed and danced in their gorgeous butterfly gowns. Nobody recognized Cinderella when she came in, but everybody gazed at her because she was the most beautiful person there. The prince came to her straight away and asked her to dance with him, and never left her side all evening.

When she saw her father leave she said she must go.

"Let me take you home then," the prince begged her, but she slipped away from him, not wanting him to know who she was. He followed after her, anxious not to lose sight of her, and she ran into the house where her father kept his doves and closed the door behind her. Then she ran through another door and out to her tree, and put her silver dress and slippers there for the birds to hide. The prince called her father out and begged him to open up the dove-house for him, but by this time Cinderella was lying in the hearth in her dirty grey dress, and nobody knew what had happened.

There was another ball the next night,

but this time Cinderella said nothing to her stepmother. She helped her sisters to get dressed and then, when they had all gone to the ball, she went out to her hazel tree.

"Hazel tree, hazel tree,
Will you help me?"

There was a rustling of leaves and the birds of the tree flew down to her, and this time her dress and her slippers shimmered like the moon. Cinderella put them on and ran to the ball, and again no one recognized her for who she was, and again the prince danced with her all night. When she left to go home she knew that he was following her, and when she was near her father's house she ran into

the garden and hid in a pear tree.

"Come down!" the prince called to her in despair. He went to her father and told him that the beautiful princess who was at the ball had hidden in the tree. The father was puzzled to think that twice the princess should hide in the grounds of his own house. He chopped down the tree, but there was nobody there, because Cinderella had taken her shimmering dress and slippers back to the hazel tree, and was lying among the ashes of the hearth in her old grey rags.

On the night of the third ball she went out again to the hazel tree.

"Hazel tree, hazel tree,
Will you help me?"

And the birds fluttered down to her with a dress and slippers that were as golden as the sun itself, and Cinderella had never looked more beautiful. The prince danced with her all night, and this time, he told himself, he would not lose her. When midnight struck and she saw that her father had left she tried to slip away. The prince ran after her instantly, calling to her to wait for him, and in her great haste she dropped one of her golden slippers. He picked it up and held it next to his heart.

"Whoever this fits, I shall marry," he said.

Next day he visited all the daughters of all the houses to have them try on the golden slipper, but it was so small and delicate that it fitted nobody. When he arrived at Cinderella's house the two ugly sisters were rubbing perfumed oils between their toes to make them smell nice.

"You have such lovely feet," their mother told them. "He's bound to marry one of you."

They scowled at each other, but when the prince came in they were full of smiles and dimples.

The oldest one tried the slipper first, but tug and push as she might she just couldn't get her foot into it. "It's my big toe!" she moaned to her mother. "It won't go in."

"Chop it off then!" her mother hissed, and handed her a knife. "You won't need it when you're married to the prince."

So she did, and the slipper fitted. But as she was riding back to the palace with the prince they passed Cinderella's hazel tree, and all the birds set up a frenzied chanting to the prince to look at her slipper.

The prince stopped the carriage and looked, and sure enough, the slipper was full of blood. He took the girl back to her mother and asked to see her sister. She did her very best to get the slipper to fit, but there didn't seem to be any chance of that.

"It's nearly there," she whispered to her mother, gasping and red-faced with the effort, "but I can't get my heel in."

"Push, you fool," her mother said, and rammed the shoe on so hard that her daughter's foot started to bleed. Still, the shoe was on, and the prince took her for his bride.

But as they were driving to the palace past the hazel tree the birds set up such a riot of chanting that the prince stopped the carriage again and saw the blood staining the heel of the sister's white stocking, so he turned the carriage round and took her back home.

"You haven't got another daughter, have you?" he said to the father.

"No," said the father, and Cinderella stood up from the ashes. "Well, only Cinderella."

"But look at the state of her," the stepmother said. "She'd never make a bride for you."

But Cinderella stepped forward and curtsied to the prince and took the slipper from his hand, and it slid on to her foot so easily that he knew it was hers. Then he looked at her face and knew that she was the girl who had danced with him for three whole nights; even though her hair was matted with ash and her clothes were stained and torn, he knew her.

The stepmother and the ugly sisters set up a great howl of rage and all the birds of the hazel tree flew down and pecked and picked at them until they sobbed for mercy and forgiveness.

But Cinderella and the prince saw nothing of this. He went down on one knee and asked her if she would marry him; and Cinderella said *yes*.

TITLES IN THE FAIRY TALE SERIES

Cinderella
BERLIE DOHERTY
Illustrated by
JANE RAY

Beauty and the Beast
BERLIE DOHERTY
Illustrated by
JANE RAY

Aladdin
BERLIE DOHERTY
Illustrated by
JANE RAY

The Frog Prince
BERLIE DOHERTY
Illustrated by
JANE RAY

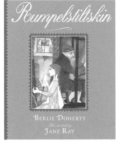

Rumpelstiltskin
BERLIE DOHERTY
Illustrated by
JANE RAY

Snow White
BERLIE DOHERTY
Illustrated by
JANE RAY

The Wild Swans
BERLIE DOHERTY
Illustrated by
JANE RAY

Rapunzel
BERLIE DOHERTY
Illustrated by
JANE RAY

Sleeping Beauty
BERLIE DOHERTY
Illustrated by
JANE RAY

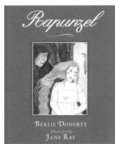

Hansel and Gretel
BERLIE DOHERTY
Illustrated by
JANE RAY

Available from all good bookstores

www.walker.co.uk

FOR THE BEST CHILDREN'S BOOKS, LOOK FOR THE BEAR.